BUTTERFLY PARK

by
Elly MacKay

RP KIDS
PHILADELPHIA · LONDON

To Lily and Koen,
Colourful and delightful . . . my little butterflies.

Books published by Running Press are available at special discounts for bulk purchases in the United States by corporations, institutions, and other organizations. For more information, please contact the Special Markets Department at the Perseus Books Group, 2300 Chestnut Street, Suite 200, Philadelphia, PA 19103, or call (800) 810-4145, ext. 5000, or e-mail special.markets@perseusbooks.com.

ISBN 978-0-7624-5339-9

Library of Congress Control Number: 2014956859

9 8 7 6 5 4 3 2 1

Digit on the right indicates the number of this printing

Designed by Frances J. Soo Ping Chow
Edited by Marlo Scrimizzi
Typography: Brandon Text and Harmon

Published by Running Press Kids
An Imprint of Running Press Book Publishers
A Member of the Perseus Books Group
2300 Chestnut Street
Philadelphia, PA 19103–4371

Visit us on the web!
www.runningpress.com/rpkids

Once there was a girl who was moving to a new town.
This made her sad. She was going to miss the birds that sang
in the morning and the crickets that sang at night.
But most of all, she was going to miss the butterflies.

After a long, winding trip . . .

. . . she and her family arrived at their new home.
Instead of birds and crickets, she heard horns and trains.

And then there was her house, plain and gray
like all the others.

GROUNDSKEEPER

721

But next to it was a gate unlike any other.
The girl repeated the letters. Suddenly, she felt very lucky!

The next morning, the girl couldn't wait to meet the butterflies.
She set off with a plate of cookies—for it was always smart
to make a good first impression.

But when she opened the gate to Butterfly Park . . .

. . . she didn't see a butterfly anywhere.

The girl waited . . .

and waited . . .

had a cookie . . .

and waited some more.

Finally, she saw one,
though it was in her neighbor's yard.

The girl knocked on their door and asked a boy
if he would help her catch the butterfly.

He agreed and knew how to reach way up high!
Together they caught the butterfly and took it to Butterfly Park.

But up, up, and away it flew over the gate.

They needed more help if they were going to bring butterflies to Butterfly Park.

So they knocked and knocked on all the neighbors' doors.

The children were happy to help. They swung their nets and caught a few.
But when they took them to Butterfly Park . . .

. . . up, up, and away the butterflies flew.

Except for one.

The children wondered what the butterfly wanted,
when suddenly . . .

. . . it flew away! The girls and boys dropped their nets
and followed the butterfly.

It took them up and down and through the town.
Curiosity grew. Windows and doors began to open.

Everyone was having such fun, others joined in too!

The butterfly led them along a winding path, and
up many twisting stairs, until they reached the top.
From there they could see . . .

. . . FLOWERS.

Yes, butterflies love flowers for their sweet nectar.
At last, the girl knew what to do!

Bright and early the next day,
she set off for Butterfly Park again . . .

. . . this time, with flowers.

The girl waited, listening to the sounds of the busy town.
There were still no butterflies.

Then, when she looked through the gate,
something caught her eye.

It was her neighbors!

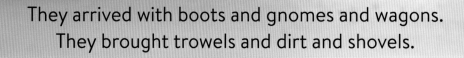

They arrived with boots and gnomes and wagons.
They brought trowels and dirt and shovels.

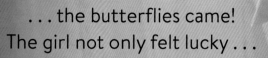

...the butterflies came!
The girl not only felt lucky...

And sure enough,

They showed her that plants need roots to grow. Together, everyone planted until the park was brimming with flowers and laughter.

in time . . .

. . . she also felt right at home.